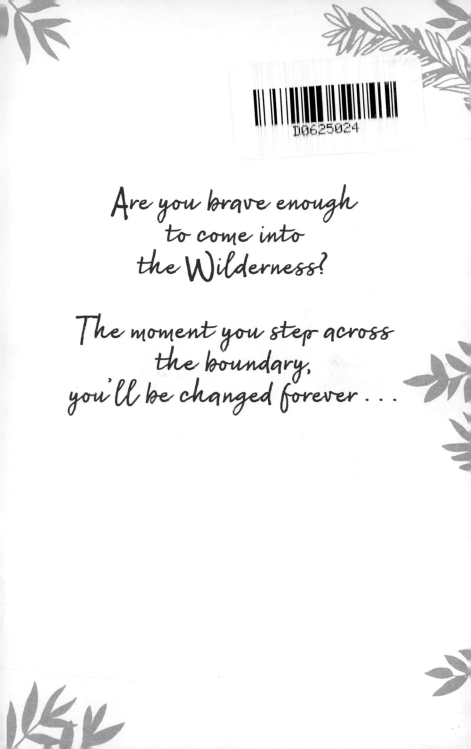

Are you brave enough
to come into
the Wilderness?

The moment you step across
the boundary,
you'll be changed forever . . .

For Vernon Oak and their kin.—G.L

For my Mum and Dad, who introduced me to the
wilderness and my own little Wildthing for whom I
hope to do the same.—R.B

OXFORD
UNIVERSITY PRESS

Great Clarendon Street, Oxford OX2 6DP
Oxford University Press is a department of the University of Oxford.
It furthers the University's objective of excellence in research, scholarship,
and education by publishing worldwide. Oxford is a registered trade mark
of Oxford University Press in the UK and in certain other countries

Text copyright © Gill Lewis 2020
Illustrations copyright © Rebecca Bagley 2020

The moral rights of the author have been asserted

Database right Oxford University Press (maker)

First published 2020

British Library Cataloguing in Publication Data

Data available

ISBN 978-0-19-277175-9

5 7 9 10 8 6 4

Printed in China

Paper used in the production of this book is a natural,
recyclable product made from wood grown in sustainable forests.
The manufacturing process conforms to the environmental
regulations of the country of origin.

Willow Wildthing
and the
Swamp Monster

Written by Gill Lewis

Illustrated by Rebecca Bagley

OXFORD
UNIVERSITY PRESS

Chapter 1
The Howling

Willow didn't know what had woken her, but she was wide awake, her eyes open and her heart banging like a drum inside her chest. Her mind spun, trying to remember where she was.

New bed.

New house.

New town.

She lay in the darkness, straining her ears to hear what had pulled her from sleep.

Water gurgled through the pipes. A clock ticked. A lorry rumbled along a road.

Moonbeams cast monster shadows on the wall behind her, and dark shapes lurked in the corners of the room.

Shivers ran down Willow's spine.

Sniff lifted his head and growled softly from the end of Willow's bed.

'What is it, Sniff?' Willow whispered. 'Did you hear something too?'

She pulled Sniff closer and held him against her chest. Sniff was a small, scruffy dog from the dog rescue centre. He had one eye, wonky teeth, and a brave heart. No one had wanted him. Everyone had passed him by, looking for cute puppies. But the moment Willow had seen him, she just knew they had to be together. It wasn't so much that Willow had chosen Sniff, but that Sniff had chosen Willow. Sniff loved her more than anything in the world.

Sniff growled softly again.

Then Willow heard what had woken her. It was a howl; a wild howl into the night. It was a low sound at first, rising to a high-pitched cry, and it was coming through the open window. Willow climbed out of bed and tiptoed across the room with Sniff in her arms. She peered out. A crescent moon spread silver light over the garden and the trees of the scrubby patch of wasteland beyond.

A wind rushed through the leaves, and the branches heaved and fell. It sounded like a storm raging across an ocean from a faraway world.

The howl rose again, wilder this time. It was a piercing cry that made Willow feel scared and lonely all at the same time.

The wind curled into Willow's bedroom and tugged at her hair. It scattered paper on her desk and lifted the curtains. It felt as if a wild thing was whirling around in her room. Sniff growled again, and Willow slammed the window shut.

Hairs prickled on the back of her neck.

Something was out there in the scrap of wasteland beyond the garden. She pulled the curtains tightly together. She wished her bedroom faced the front of the house instead of the woods. She thought about climbing into bed with Mum and Dad, but she knew they were tired. They had been at the hospital all day with her little brother,

Freddie. She climbed back into her own
bed and fell into a restless sleep where she
dreamed she was lost in a deep dark forest.
She dreamed she was running and running,
chased by monsters that hid in the shadows.
Worst of all, however hard she searched, she
just couldn't find Freddie.

Chapter 2
Dognapped

Willow woke again to bright sunlight. She opened the curtains and peered out.

The summer sky was blue with puffy white clouds drifting high above. Below her, the garden stretched away to two old gnarled apple trees at the far end. Clothes flapped on the washing line, and somewhere an ice cream van tinkled its tune.

It was hard to imagine the howling last night. Had she dreamed it?

She could hear the clattering of plates in the kitchen and went downstairs, with Sniff following closely at her heels.

Mum and Dad were busy emptying boxes and trying to find places to put things in their new house.

'Hello, sleepyhead,' said Dad.

Mum looked at the clock. 'It's almost lunchtime. Didn't you get much sleep?'

'Not much,' said Willow. 'Did you hear anything last night?'

'Like what?' said Mum.

A monster was what she wanted to say, but it sounded so silly now. 'It's nothing,' she said, but she couldn't help looking out at the wood beyond the footpath at the bottom of the garden. Trees rose up, tall and scraggly above the thickets of bramble and nettles. It looked scary and dark, and Willow decided that she would never set foot in there. Ever. 'What's in that wood?' she asked.

'It's not exactly a wood,' said Dad. 'It's the gardens and grounds of an old house that burned down long ago. It's a bit of a wasteland in the town now. It's a mess. It's overgrown with weeds. I've heard people dump rubbish in there too. It needs a good tidy-up.'

'It'd be nice if it could be made into a park,' said Mum.

'I expect houses will be built there,' said Dad. 'It needs something doing to it.'

Willow stared down towards the scrubby patch of land. Brambles lay like thick coils of barbed wire on the other side of the ditch, as if the wasteland was trying to keep people out.

'I'm off to see Freddie soon,' said Mum.

'Can I come with you? asked Willow.

'I've got an appointment with his doctor this afternoon. But you can come with me tomorrow,' said Mum. 'He'll love to see you.'

Willow sighed. Freddie was nearly three years old, but he had been poorly since he had been born and sometimes needed to stay in hospital. Willow's mum and dad had decided to move to a new house to be closer to the hospital so that they could all be together.

'What will you do today?' asked Mum.

Willow shrugged her shoulders. If she were back in their old house, she'd play with her friends in the park. She didn't know anyone here.

Mum smiled. 'Well, you've got Dad all to yourself today.'

Dad sat down in an old armchair and yawned. 'We could explore the garden. Why don't you get an old sheet we can string up between the branches of the apple trees and make a den?'

Willow said goodbye to Mum and went to her bedroom to fetch her rucksack. She hadn't spent much time with Dad for ages because he had been busy with work and the move and hospital visits seeing Freddie. Today it would be just the two of them. She had Dad all to herself. She packed her skipping rope and fleecy bedcover to make a tent den and went downstairs to find him.

But Dad was in the armchair, snoring loudly.

'Dad?' she said.

Dad didn't even move. He was fast asleep.

She thought about waking him but didn't want to bother him. She decided to let him rest.

Willow sighed. 'It's just you and me again, Sniff.'

'Uff!' agreed Sniff.

Willow walked down to the end of the garden with Sniff running ahead, his nose to the ground. The garden was long and thin with the two gnarled apple trees at the end where grasses grew tall and wild.

It didn't seem much fun building the den by herself. Her school friends were far, far away in another town. Maybe one day she

could build a den with Freddie. She sighed.
She wished she could take the garden to
Freddie.

Maybe she could, she thought. She could
collect things from the new garden and show
them to him.

Willow began searching for garden
treasures.

She pulled a dandelion and blew the seeds
into the air. She wished again for Freddie to
be out of hospital, and for Mum and Dad to
be happy and not worried all the time. She
watched her wishes drift up, up, and away.

She remembered last night's dream of
being chased by monsters and losing Freddie.
The dark made everything more frightening.

'No monsters,' she called to Sniff.

But Sniff wasn't listening. He was looking

into the hedge at the bottom of the garden.

A low growl rose in his throat.

'What is it, Sniff?' whispered Willow.

Sniff moved closer, sniffing at the hedge.
Something large was moving behind it.
Twigs snapped. Dry leaves rustled.

'Sniff!' called Willow.

The whole hedge seemed to bend
towards Sniff.

Willow jumped to her feet. 'Sniff, come
back.'

'Uff!' Barked Sniff. 'Grrr . . . uff.'

Willow blinked once and saw something
reach out from the hedge and grab hold of
Sniff.

Willow blinked twice.

And Sniff was gone.

Chapter 3
Piranhas and Crocodiles

'Sniff!'

Willow jumped to her feet and scrambled through the gap in the hedge where Sniff had disappeared.

She looked down the path that ran along the back of the gardens to see four children running away, taking Sniff with them.

'Hey, stop!' she yelled, but it just seemed to make the children run even faster.

Willow glanced back at the house. There

was no time to call Dad. She set off after the children.

To one side lay the safety of houses and neat gardens. To the other lay the wild wooded wasteland. It was separated from the path by a ditch filled with green stagnant water. Crisp packets and drink cans bobbed on its surface.

The children came to a stop at last, but then Willow saw them trot single file across a plank over the ditch. Once on the other side, they pulled a rope and drew the plank up like a drawbridge.

There was no way she could get across.

Willow stopped to face them. 'Give my dog back.'

The four children were all very grubby and were covered in bits of woodland. Moss and sticks and feathers were

stuck in their hair
and clothes.

'Who are you?' demanded Willow.

The smallest of them turned to the one holding Sniff. 'Don't tell her your name, Fox.'

Fox spun round to look at the small one. 'You idiot, Mouse. Now she knows.'

Willow folded her arms. 'I know two of your names now,' she said.

The tallest figure stepped forward. She had dark black hair and a cloak that folded around her like black wings. 'I'm Raven,' she said. She pointed to the fourth figure who was bouncing up and down on the spot. 'And this is Hare. We are the Wild Things. Who are you?'

'I'm Willow,' said Willow. 'And you've got my dog.'

'We need to borrow him for a mission,' said Fox. 'We'll bring him back.'

'If we do get back, that is,' added Hare.

'We might get gobbled by the swamp monster,' added Mouse.

'I want Sniff back now,' demanded Willow. 'You put that plank back across the ditch so I can get him.'

'Can't do that, sorry,' said Fox. 'We need him. We can't allow you to cross Green Slime River.'

'Sniff will be scared without me,' said Willow. She looked at Sniff and didn't want to admit that he didn't look scared. In fact, he looked like he was enjoying himself. He licked Fox on the face and wagged his tail.

'We have to go now,' said Raven. 'And we have to borrow your dog. We apologize for the inconvenience.'

Willow could feel tears well up. She brushed them away with her sleeve and glared at Raven. 'If you don't put that plank back now, then I'm swimming across,' she said.

Hare peered into the slimy water. 'You don't want to do that. There's piranhas in there.'

'What's piranhas?' said Mouse. He leaned forward and peered in too.

'They're fish with razor-sharp teeth that strip you to the bones in five seconds flat,' said Hare.

'Yeah,' said Mouse, looking impressed. 'There's crocodiles too. You won't be anything but bones by the time they've finished with you.' He blew a raspberry at

Willow to make his point.

Willow looked down into the murky water. She didn't believe their silly stories, but she didn't want to wade across. It looked slimy and horrible. Besides, she didn't know how deep it was. She slid a little way down the bank and looked up at them. 'Well, you've got my dog, so I'm coming whether you like it or not. And if I do get munched, you can carry my bones back to my mum and dad and tell them why you didn't let me over your bridge.'

The Wild Things all looked at each other. This wasn't quite what they had in mind.

'She does have a point,' said Hare. 'Carrying bones back could be rather messy.'

'Time for a Wild Squawk,' said Fox.

The Wild Things huddled in a circle, and all Willow could hear were harsh whispers. From time to time a Wild Thing would look up and glance in her direction and scowl.

Then the Wild Things stood in a line again.

Fox seemed to be the spokesperson. 'All the Wild Things agree . . .'

Raven coughed loudly at this. 'Not all . . .'

Fox glared at Raven and began again. 'Most of the Wild Things agree that, as Sniff is your dog, you can come with us.'

'But only on one condition,' said Raven. She stood up tall and put her hand on her heart. 'You must promise to never tell anyone about the Wilderness.'

'The Wilderness?' said Willow.

'Yeah,' said Mouse. 'If you break the promise, crows will peck out your eyeballs.' He blew another loud raspberry because it seemed the right thing to do.

'What's the Wilderness?' asked Willow.

'The Wilderness is everything between the unexplored Forest of Forever Night in the west and the Dragon Gardens in the east,' said Hare.

Willow folded her arms. 'It's just a wood,' she said. 'It's not even that big.' She remembered her dad's words. 'It's a mess. It needs a good tidy-up.'

Mouse gasped and looked at the others.

Hare stepped forward, glancing over her shoulder as if the trees were listening. 'This isn't just any wood,' she whispered.

Fox nodded. 'There are mountains, deep

ravines, and fast rivers in here.'

Willow laughed. 'That's impossible.'

Raven narrowed her eyes. 'You know everything, do you?'

'No,' said Willow. Something about Raven made her doubt herself. 'It's just that it doesn't look that big.'

'Strange things happen in here,' said Hare. 'Time bends and stretches. This place is as big as you want it to be.'

'It holds more than you could possibly imagine,' said Fox.

Mouse glanced back at the trees. 'There's even a witch.'

Willow stared into the wood. A wind flowed through the trees, and dark shadows slipped across the forest floor. A howl rose up from somewhere deep in the Wilderness.

It was a raw sound of pain and anger. Willow thought there was sadness in the howl too.

'There's also a monster,' said Mouse.

Willow swallowed hard. So the howl she had heard the night before was real. 'You can't scare me that easily,' she said. 'I'm not leaving Sniff. I'm coming with you.'

Raven folded her arms, wrapping the wings of her cloak around herself. 'Are you sure you're brave enough? Because the moment you step across this bridge, you'll be changed forever.'

Chapter 4
Outsiders

'I'm not going without my dog,' said Willow.

'OK,' said Fox. He released the rope holding the plank and lowered it across the ditch.

Willow took a step on to the bridge.

Raven stepped on to the other end and spread the wings of her cape wide, blocking the way. 'You have to take your shoes off. It's the rules. You can't be a Wild Thing wearing shoes.'

'Not in summer anyway,' said Mouse.

'You can put them with the others under that bush,' said Fox.

'I'll get muddy feet,' said Willow. 'Mum will be cross.'

Raven shrugged her shoulders. 'It's the rules.'

Willow slipped off her trainers and socks and pushed them under the bush. She counted five other pairs of shoes there. Yet there were only four Wild Things on the other side of the bridge.

'Why are there five pairs of shoes and only four of you?' asked Willow.

Mouse stepped forward. 'They belong to . . .'

'Shut up, Mouse,' snapped Raven. She glared at Willow. 'Well, are you coming or not?'

35

'Uff!' barked Sniff.

Willow took another step on the bridge, feeling the cool, rough surface of the plank of wood against her feet. The light in the forest seemed to become a little brighter. Birdsong fell from the trees, calling her in.

She glanced into the water underneath her. Green scum lay on its surface. It was dark and murky. A shopping trolley lay half submerged. An old rotten log bobbed under the bridge. It's just a log, she told herself. That's all. But as she stepped across the bridge, the log seemed to slide beneath her. It rolled on to its side and, for a moment, Willow couldn't tell if she saw a line of white fungus or a row of gleaming white, very sharp teeth. It seemed to follow her to the end of the bridge and then disappeared

under the slime. Big bubbles rose from the depths and burst at the water's surface.

Mouse was staring at her. 'Told you there were crocodiles.'

Willow looked at Mouse. There was something different about him. He twitched his nose, and his eyes darted about looking for danger.

'Are you sure you want to come?' said Raven. She put her head to one side. 'You look a bit scared to me.'

Willow turned to look at Raven. She looked a bit different too. The edges of her cape ruffled in the breeze like feathers.

'It's not too late to go back,' said Hare. 'We're going to the Wilderness, where anything can happen.'

Willow glanced back across Green Slime

River and the safety of the footpath on the other side of the bridge. She could go home, but that would mean leaving Sniff. There was something else too. It drifted through the forest on the breeze. It lifted the ends of her hair, and it seemed to whisper the promise of adventure.

How could she refuse?

Sniff barked and struggled in Fox's arms. Even Fox seemed a bit more foxy. Hare bounced up and down on her long legs, ready to run. The harder Willow stared, the more they seemed to be a curious mix of child and creature. They looked as if they had the wild in them.

'I want my dog,' said Willow, eyeing them warily.

'Then you'll have to come with us,' said

Fox. He nodded to Raven, who pulled on the rope, lifting up the bridge.

Fox put Sniff on the ground, and the small dog bounded over to Willow, jumping around her in excitement.

She pulled him into her arms, and he licked her face. 'I'm not sure what this place is, Sniff,' she whispered, 'but it seems we're about to find out, whether we like it or not.'

'Uff!' woofed Sniff softly. 'Uff!'

'Quiet!' squawked Raven. 'Outsiders!'

Willow felt herself pulled to the ground behind a thorn bush.

'Keep down,' hissed Hare.

Willow peered through the spiky brambles.

'Don't let them see us,' whispered Fox.

A man and a woman were walking along

the path.

'Who are Outsiders?' whispered Willow.

'People who can't see the Wilderness,' whispered Hare. 'Adults mainly. They don't know it's here. All they see is a mess they want to tidy up.'

'Why can't they see it?' said Willow.

Hare looked at her. 'Have you ever met an adult that believes in magic?'

'I'm not sure *I* believe in magic either,' said Willow.

Hare leaned closer. 'There's magic in here. It'll seep into you, whether you think you want it or not.'

Fox stood up and brushed the dirt from his knees. 'They're gone. Let's get to River Camp before any more Outsiders come.' He led the way into a dark tunnel made from thorns and brambles.

'This is the entrance to the Wilderness,' whispered Mouse. 'It's the Holloway. It's the only way in.'

Hare stopped to stare up at the sky. 'South,' she muttered.

Willow looked up too, but all she could see were the tops of the trees and puffy white clouds drifting by. 'What are you looking at?'

Hare shook her head. 'Nothing.'

'Come on,' called Raven.

Willow glanced back one last time, leaving the rows of houses and the neat gardens behind her. She turned and scrambled after the Wild Things through the Holloway, deeper and deeper into the Wilderness, and she began to wonder what sort of world lay waiting for her ahead.

Chapter 5
River Camp

The tunnel of thorns became narrower and narrower until Willow had to wriggle on her belly to get through. She was relieved to be able to follow the others out on the other side. She stood up, wiped her muddy hands on her jeans, and stared around her. The scrubby woodland seemed bigger than she had thought it would be. The trees seemed taller too. Sunlight filtered down through the leaves in shafts of yellow and gold. The air smelled cool and damp, and the hum of traffic was replaced by birdsong.

They were standing on the edge of a steep slope, looking down into a small valley where a river curled around the base of an old oak tree.

'Is this the Wilderness?' whispered Willow.

Raven scowled. 'You mustn't tell anyone about this place, remember? It's ours. It's our secret.'

Hare stepped to the edge and looked back over her shoulder. 'But it's not safe any more. There's a new danger,' she said. 'There's a monster in the Wilderness.' She paused for a moment, sniffing the air.

Willow's eyes opened wide as Hare took a step over the edge and disappeared. Raven and Fox did the same. Willow crept to the edge and watched them sliding down the slope, the dry leaves flying up behind them.

'Uff!' barked Sniff, and he leapt after them, his little legs spinning beneath him.

Willow stared after them. It looked much too steep and scary.

'I'm not brave enough either,' said Mouse quietly. 'I'm going down the Root Ladder. You can follow me.'

Willow followed Mouse down the slope, holding on to the gnarled roots of a tree. At the bottom, she could see a small clearing beside the river and a ring of stones around a campfire.

'This is River Camp,' said Mouse as they joined Fox, Raven, Hare and Scruff. He turned to Willow and beamed. 'It's the best place in the whole world.'

A thin line of smoke rose from the ashes of the fire. Water burbled over stones in the river, and small birds flitted through the branches. Despite the peaceful scene, Willow could see that something was very wrong. A wooden den lay in ruins. Sticks supporting an old tarpaulin had been pulled to the ground. Pots and pans were scattered around the campfire.

Fox peered into the ruined den. 'It's worse than we thought.'

Willow looked in too. Clothes and books had been tossed around and covered in thick lumps of mud. A large blob of something red and sticky lay at the entrance.

'Blood?' said Willow.

Fox frowned and shook his head. 'Strawberry jam.'

Mouse gripped Willow's hand. 'It was the swamp monster. He took our jam doughnuts.'

'The swamp monster?' said Willow.

Hare started picking up the overturned pots. 'We knew things weren't right. Things have been going missing for a while. Biscuits, cakes, chocolate. Fox lost his penknife, and I lost my compass. It always happened when we weren't here.'

Fox pulled out a large round biscuit tin from under a blanket, opened it, and peered in. 'Our emergency chocolate is still here,' he said. 'The swamp monster hasn't taken that.' He put the tin safely on a tree stump.

'We thought the thief lived in the Forest of Forever Night,' said Raven. 'We traced some prints there, and so Fox, Hare, and I went on an expedition to find out.'

Hare put an arm around Mouse's shoulders. 'But the swamp monster came into camp when we were out. Mouse saw it happen.'

Mouse nodded and sniffed. 'It was just Bear and me here.'

'Bear?' said Willow.

'Bear's one of us. He's a Wild Thing too,' said Mouse. 'We were getting the fire ready to make hot chocolate for the others.' He buried his face in Hare's shoulder, remembering the terrible moment. 'It came out of nowhere. It was a huge hairy ball of mud with fangs.'

Fox dipped his finger in the jam and sniffed it. 'Mouse said the monster jumped on him and tried to eat him, but Bear managed to pull it away. It grabbed a bag full of jam doughnuts and ran off.'

Mouse peeped out. 'Bear was so mad at that. He loves food. Especially doughnuts. He ran after the monster, and we haven't seen Bear since. We don't even know where he is.'

Willow looked at the ruined camp. 'How big is this monster?'

Mouse turned to face Willow, his eyes growing wider and wider. 'Bigger than big.'

Fox knelt down and pointed to something on the ground. 'Mouse is right,' he said. 'It's massive.'

Willow and the Wild Things gathered around to look. There was a monster paw print in the mud. It was bigger than Willow's hand, and there were four long claw marks scratched deep into the earth.

Chapter 6
The Witch's Lair

'How do you think Sniff can help you?'
asked Willow.

'It's my idea,' said Raven. She picked up
an old jumper from the ground. 'This is
Bear's jumper. Sniff can smell Bear's scent
and follow his trail.'

Willow frowned. 'He's never done that
before. He might not know how.'

Fox folded his arms. 'That's exactly what
I said.' He turned to Raven. 'See? I told you

it wouldn't work.'

Raven held the jumper against Sniff's nose, and Sniff sniffed it. 'Now go find Bear.'

To Willow's surprise, Sniff put his nose to the ground and started walking in ever widening circles around the camp. When he reached the huge paw print, he set off following the river downstream.

He stopped and looked back at them all. 'Uff!' he barked. *This way.*

'See!' said Raven, turning to Fox. 'I told you my idea was the best.'

Fox scowled. 'If you hadn't got us lost on our expedition into the Forest of Forever Night, we would've been back in time to help Bear.'

'It was dark in the forest,' snapped Raven.

'You said you knew where you were going,' said Fox.

'I did!' insisted Raven.

'Until you got lost,' muttered Fox. 'Hare had to find the way back.'

'Uff!' barked Sniff impatiently. 'Uff!'

'Stop wasting time,' said Hare. 'Sniff wants us to follow him.'

Raven swished her cloak. 'Let's go.'

'Wait,' said Fox. 'Let's think what we might need. Hare is the map-maker and we might discover new lands.'

Hare rummaged through the den and brought out a large scroll of paper hidden inside a cardboard tube. 'Luckily the monster didn't take the map.'

Raven picked up her catapult and wiped
the mud from it.

Mouse knelt down and picked up two pieces of wood. 'The monster broke my sword,' he wailed. 'I can't fight without it.'

'We have to go,' snapped Raven. 'Come on.'

'Can I make another one?' said Mouse.

'There's no time,' said Fox. 'I'll lead the way.'

'This was my idea,' said Raven, pushing to the front. 'I'll go first.'

Willow and the Wild Things followed Sniff alongside the river. Sniff kept his nose to the ground, following Bear's trail deeper and deeper into the woods.

Willow stayed at the back with Mouse. 'Do Fox and Raven always argue like that?'

Mouse nodded. 'Always. They both think they're always right.'

'Wait,' whispered Hare, as they reached a bend in the river. 'We haven't been beyond here before. I need to draw this on the map so we can find our way back.' She pulled out the map and a pencil and stared at the sky. 'We're heading north.'

'How can you tell without your compass?' asked Willow.

Hare shrugged her shoulders. 'I read the wild signs in here.'

'What are the wild signs?' asked Willow.

'Only Hare knows,' whispered Mouse.

Willow frowned. 'But why can't Hare tell us?'

'Because,' said Hare, turning to glare at Willow, 'reading wild signs is an ancient art. You wouldn't understand.'

Willow leaned over to look at the map,

but Raven stood in the way.

'The map of the Wilderness is secret,' said Raven. 'Only Wild Things are allowed to look.'

Hare finished drawing and rolled up the map. 'Come on. We'll bend twigs to mark our path back.'

Willow and the Wild Things walked on, with Hare bending twigs and leaving sticks as arrow markers on the ground.

Hare stopped from time to time to look at the tracks. 'The monster has definitely come this way,' she said, pointing to claw marks in the earth. 'And these are Bear's footprints. But look! There are other prints too.'

Willow crouched down to examine the prints of a pair of boots.

'They look fresh,' said Fox.

Mouse clung to Fox's arm. 'And look where they go!'

The boot prints left the path and headed through trees to a small hut in a clearing. Steam rose from a blackened pot hung over the fire, and a strange blue light glowed from within the hut.

'It's the witch's hut,' whispered Mouse.

'So this is where she lives,' said Hare. She unrolled the map to mark it on there. 'We've heard her in the woods before.'

'CAW! CAW! CAW!'

A large crow landed on a branch beside them 'CAW! CAW! CAW!'

'Uff! Uff!' barked Sniff.

The hut door flung open, and the witch stood in the doorway, silhouetted by the blue light. 'Who's there?' she croaked.

'Shh!' said Fox.

The crow bobbed up and down on the branch. 'Caw! Caw!'

'I know someone's there,' called the witch. She stepped out into the light of the clearing and began shuffling towards the Wild Things.

Willow crept back into the shadows. She had never seen a real witch before. This was a short, plump witch, with wild yellow hair. And she was coming their way.

'Run,' yelled Raven.

And Willow found her feet flying along after the Wild Things, following the river, deeper and deeper into the forest.

Chapter 7
Valley of the Killer Plants

Willow and the Wild Things stopped to catch their breath. They were all puffing and panting.

'I recognized the witch,' said Fox.

'Me too,' said Mouse, looking back along the path. 'She's the writer who came to talk to our school.'

Raven narrowed her eyes. 'A clever disguise, when all along on to she's really a witch.'

'Uff!' barked Sniff, trotting along the path.

'Come on,' said Fox. 'We've got to find Bear.'

The river cut deeper and deeper into the earth until it tumbled over a waterfall down into a steep ravine. Willow peered over. The water churned and frothed and sent up a fine spray of mist. It seemed to lie far, far below, and Willow wondered again at how the small scrubby piece of wasteland could hide such a vast wilderness. Sniff ran on until he stopped beside a huge tree that had fallen across from one side of the ravine to the other. He sniffed a few times and then trotted across.

Hare leapt after him, followed by Fox and Raven.

Mouse took a step on to the tree trunk. He looked down and froze. 'I can't do it,' he

whispered to Willow. 'It's too high up.'

Willow looked down too. Far below, the bottom was carpeted with strange plants with huge leaves that swished as if creatures were moving around beneath them.

'Come on over, Mouse,' called Raven. She made her way back across the tree trunk.

Mouse climbed back on to the ground. His bottom lip wobbled. 'I can't.'

Raven rolled her eyes. 'I told Fox we should have left you at camp. You're too young and too small.'

Fox walked back over the log. 'What's the matter?'

'Mouse is scared,' said Raven.

'Mouse!' said Fox irritably. 'You'll have to cross.'

'I can't,' said Mouse. He began backing away.

'We have to save Bear,' said Raven. 'And you're not helping.'

Mouse burst into tears.

'This is your fault, Fox,' said Raven. 'You'll have to stay with him.'

'I'm not going back,' said Fox. 'I'm leading this rescue.'

'This rescue was my idea,' snapped Raven.

Hare leapt across and held out her hands. 'Come on, Mouse. You can do it. Come with me.'

But Mouse shook his head. 'I can't.'

Raven turned to Mouse. 'You'll have to go back to camp.'

Mouse's eyes opened wide. 'What if the monster goes back to the camp too?'

'One of us has to go with him,' said Hare. 'I can't because I'm the map maker.'

Fox and Raven glared at each other. Neither wanted to go back with Mouse. They both wanted to lead this mission.

Willow could see tears form in Mouse's eyes. She knew what it felt like to be left out of things. She put an arm around him. 'I'll go back with Mouse.'

'Fine,' said Raven.

'Are you sure?' said Hare.

Willow nodded.

Sniff crossed back and sat next to Willow. 'Uff!' He didn't want to leave her.

'Come on, Sniff,' whistled Fox. 'We need you.'

Willow bent down and scratched his ears. 'You have to help them find Bear,' she said. 'Go on. Go.'

Sniff gave her hand a lick and then followed the others across the fallen tree.

'Look after Sniff for me,' called Willow, but the other Wild Things and Sniff were already out of sight.

Mouse sat down and covered his face with his hands. 'They're cross with me because I'm too scared. I've let everyone down.'

'No you haven't,' said Willow. She secretly thought the others had let Mouse down by leaving him. She bent down and hugged him. She thought of Freddie and how brave he was even when he was scared. 'Don't worry, Mouse. Courage is often found when you need it most.'

Mouse looked up at her. 'How will I know when I find it?'

'You'll know,' said Willow. 'Maybe we can find another way and follow the others. We could scramble down to the bottom of the ravine and up the other side.'

'No one's been to the bottom of the ravine,' said Mouse. 'Fox said there are killer plants down there.'

'We could go a little way and see,' said Willow. 'We could be the first to explore it.'

'I would if I had my sword,' said Mouse, 'but the monster broke it.'

Willow held out her hand. 'Let's go back to River Camp. We can wait for the others there.'

She pulled Mouse to his feet, but he stumbled and landed face down on the ground.

He sat up and pulled at the fallen

branch that had tripped him. 'Stupid thing!' He tugged at it, and part of it broke away in his hand. Willow turned to see Mouse staring at a long stick. His mouth was wide open, and he had a look of wonder on his face.

The stick had split to show a pale greenish wood, and it came to a very fine pointy tip. Mouse held it by the other end, which had thick rough bark for a good grip. 'A sword,' he said, his eyes shining. 'My very own sword. It's better than my last one.'

Mouse stood at the top of the ravine, staring down into the Valley of the Killer Plants. He turned to Willow. 'I think it's found me,' he said.

'What has?' said Willow.

'Courage,' said Mouse, wielding his sword above his head. 'Come on. I'll lead the way.'

Chapter 8
Monster Slayer

Willow and Mouse found a route down the ravine holding on to the roots of trees. When they came to the bottom, Mouse paused. The plants grew up over their heads. Huge umbrella-like leaves created a green gloom. As they walked forward, the plants grew closer together and brushed against Willow's legs. The air was still and damp. It was cold too—a sort of cold that made her bones feel heavy. Things scuttled through the undergrowth alongside them.

The hairs on the back of Willow's neck prickled. It felt as if something was watching them.

Mouse held his sword out in front of them.

Huge snails looped their slimy trails over the leaves. Willow picked up an empty snail shell from the ground and turned it over in her hand. Freddie might want to look at it. She slipped it in her pocket and stood up.

A breath of wind blew on Willow's back.

'Ow!' cried Willow. 'Something bit me.'

She rubbed her arm to see red bumps rising on her bare skin. She turned to look but couldn't see anything hiding among the leaves.

'Ow!' cried Mouse. 'Me too.'

Willow felt more bites on her bare ankles. She looked down to see a jagged leaf brush against her. It had rows of tiny, razor-sharp teeth.

'Don't move,' cried Mouse. 'It's the plants. They're biting us.'

The wind blew, and another lunged at her from the front and then from behind.

Mouse slashed at them with his sword. 'Come on, run.' He ran ahead but a green tendril tripped him. He fell, almost dropping his sword. Another plant caught Willow by the hair. The more she struggled, the more she could feel its thorns dig into her scalp.

'Mouse!'

Mouse scrambled to his feet. He slashed left and right with his sword, slicing through stems and creepers, chopping them into pieces.

Mouse grabbed Willow's hand. 'Come on. Let's get out of here!'

The plants' creepers and tendrils tried to curl around them and trip them as they ran, but they leapt across stones in the river and scrambled up the other side of the ravine.

Once they were away from the plants, Willow stopped to rub her skin. 'That was very brave of you, Mouse,' she said. 'You got us out of there.'

'It was the sword,' Mouse said, admiring it. 'This saved us in the Valley of the Killer Plants, and this sword will save us from the swamp monster too.'

Willow took the sword from Mouse. 'Kneel down, Mouse.'

Mouse frowned and kneeled.

Then Willow held the sword up high.

'Henceforth,' she said grandly, 'this sword shall be known as Monster Slayer.' She touched the blade on Mouse's shoulders. 'Arise, Mouse, keeper of the Monster Slayer.'

Mouse beamed. 'I can't wait to tell the others. I wonder where they are.'

Willow looked into the dark trees. Cold fingers of mist curled through the forest and around her, making her shiver. 'We don't have a map,' she said.

'OOOOOOWWWWWWOOOOO!' The howl rose up ahead of them.

'This way,' said Mouse, following the sound. 'If we want to find the others, we'll have to find the monster.'

Willow heard Sniff's excited barks before she saw him. He came bounding towards her and then led her and Mouse to the others, who were standing by the edge of a vast swamp.

Raven, Hare, and Fox turned around.

'You found us,' said Raven.

Mouse held his sword up high. 'We were the first to enter the Valley of the Killer Plants. This is my sword, the Monster Slayer.'

Raven peered at it, impressed.

'It's a good sword,' said Hare.

'Well, we're going to need it,' said Fox. 'We know where the monster lives.'

'Where?' said Willow.

'Skull Rock,' said Fox. He pointed to the monster paw prints that disappeared into the mud. 'Bear must be in there too.'

On the far side of the bog, rising above the mist, sat a large skull-shaped rock with a yawning cave mouth.

'Grrrrrrr…' warned Sniff. 'Uff! Uff!'

A howl came from inside the cave.

'AWWWWOOOOOOOOOOOOOOOO!'

The sound filled Willow's head and made her chest ache. She felt as if she were lost and abandoned and alone in the world.

The Wild Things huddled closer together.

Only Mouse stood at the swamp edge, facing the cave, defiantly holding Monster Slayer high up the air.

Chapter 9
Will-o'-the-wisp

'What do we do now?' asked Willow.

'We have no choice,' said Fox. 'We have to rescue Bear.'

The swamp stretched out in front of them. Pools of oily black water lay on the gloopy mud. It bubbled and burped foul stinking gas as if it were a living thing.

The mist had crept across the ground, surrounding them in a white veil.

'We'll have to go back and find another

way across,' said Raven.

'It's too far,' said Fox. 'We have to cross here.'

'Don't be stupid,' said Raven. 'It's too dangerous.'

'I agree with Raven. We don't know how deep the bog is,' said Hare.

'There must be a way,' said Fox. 'Bear and the monster came this way.' He walked to the edge of the swamp, and his feet sank a little into the mud. He glanced back at Raven and Hare and scowled. Raven and Hare thought they knew everything. Well, he'd show them. He'd find a way across and prove them wrong. He stared out over the bog again and saw a little blue flame shimmering in the mist. It danced over the mud, away from him and back again. It seemed to be showing him the way.

He took a step on to the bog where the little light danced. The bog held his weight. He turned to the others. 'It's this way.'

'Fox!' yelled Raven. 'Come back.'

Fox took another step and another, and the mud felt quite firm beneath him. A whole line of blue flames lit up, showing a path across. 'See,' he called to Raven. 'I told you.'

Fox followed the line of blue flames, but suddenly they all flickered and went out. The mud beneath Fox gave a big stinky burp, and Fox felt the ground disappear beneath him.

'Help!' shouted Fox, as the mud began rising over his knees. But the harder he tried to move, the deeper he sank.

'I'm coming!' yelled Raven, wading out to him.

She didn't get far before she began sinking in the mud too.

Mouse held out his sword. 'Try to grab it,' he called.

But Fox and Raven were too far away. The bog bubbled and slurped as Fox and Raven sank deeper and deeper.

'Stop struggling,' shouted Hare. 'It's making it worse.'

'We need a rope,' shouted Raven. 'We should have brought a rope.'

'I've got a rope!' cried Willow. She remembered the skipping rope she had packed. She pulled off her rucksack and reached in for the rope. She held one end and threw the other to Raven, who was nearest. Raven held on to one end, and Hare, Willow, and Mouse pulled the other.

Even Sniff took hold and pulled Raven out.

Willow threw the rope to Fox, and together they hauled him out too.

'I told you,' said Raven. 'It's too dangerous.'

'Bear must've come this way,' said Fox. 'The monster's prints go through the swamp.'

'Bear's don't,' said Hare.

The Wild Things turned to look at her.

'Bear's prints go around the edge of the swamp,' said Hare.

'Come on then,' said Raven.

Sniff picked up Bear's scent, and they followed him until they reached a huge weeping willow tree. Sniff circled a few times, then stopped and whined.

'He's lost the scent,' said Willow.

Hare bent down and looked for Bear's footprints. 'They just stop,' she said. 'It's as if he's disappeared into thin air.'

'Which is exactly what he has done,' said Raven, pointing above them.

Willow looked to see the long drooping branches of the weeping willow tree.

'He's swung across,' said Fox. He turned to the others. 'We'll have to too.'

'I'll try,' said Hare. She tested out the strength of a willow branch and then swung across, dropping down on the other side.

The others followed, with Willow carrying Sniff in her rucksack.

Fox turned to face the cave entrance. 'Bear,' he called. 'Bear! It's us, the Wild Things.'

'BEAR!' called Raven. 'We've come to save you.'

Sniff gave a warning growl.

Something stirred inside the cave. A huge walking mass of swamp filled the entrance. It stank of rotting plants and boiled cabbage. Water dripped from its mouth, and it stared at them from dark, sludge-coloured eyes.

There was no sign of Bear.

And the swamp monster looked very, very hungry.

Chapter 10
Mouse's Last Stand

High on the ledge above the cave entrance, Bear peered over.

'Run while you can!' yelled Bear.

'You're alive!' shouted Hare.

'What happened?' called Fox.

Bear sat up on the ledge and peered nervously down. 'I followed the monster to the cave and tried to get the doughnuts back, but it tried to drag me in there too.'

'Did it try to eat you?' asked Mouse.

'It didn't get a chance,' said Bear. 'I picked up one of the doughnuts and lobbed it into the back of the cave. It let go of me and ran after it. So I climbed up here.'

'That was quick thinking,' said Raven.

'You've got to go,' said Bear. 'If I come down, it'll get me before I can reach you.'

'I've got my catapult,' said Raven. 'I'll fire stones at it.'

Hare put her hand on Raven's arm. 'You might hit Bear.'

'I've got Monster Slayer,' said Mouse. 'I'll save Bear.'

Before anyone could stop him, Mouse was running towards the cave, his sword held high.

'Uff! Uff! Uff!' barked Sniff.

'Come and meet the Monster Slayer,' challenged Mouse.

'No! Mouse!' yelled Willow.

The swamp monster bounded towards Mouse. Its wide-open mouth showed a row of sharp gleaming fangs. Mouse wielded his sword, but the monster clamped the sword in its teeth. It shook it, but Mouse clung on. Then the monster began dragging Mouse into the cave.

'Let go' hollered Hare.

'Mouse!' yelled Raven.

'Drop the sword,' shouted Fox.

But Willow knew that Mouse would never give up his sword. Mouse was dragged deeper and deeper into the cave, kicking and screaming until the darkness swallowed him up.

Mouse's cry filled the cave, and then stopped, quite suddenly.

In its place was a terrible, deathly silence.

Chapter 11
The Witch's Cauldron

There was silence except for the sound of *splosh, splosh, CAW! Splosh, splosh, CAW!*

Out of the mist came the witch, with the crow flying by her side.

Willow shrank back against the others.

The witch pulled back her hood and scowled at them. Her wild yellow hair seemed to glow in the mist, and her face was leathery and wrinkled. Her baggy tie-dyed trousers were stuffed into a pair of purple welly boots. The crow settled on her shoulder.

'What's all this noise?' snapped the witch.

The Wild Things looked at each other, not daring to speak.

She took a step closer. 'Well?'

The crow tipped his head to the side and glared at them. 'CAW!'

Raven stepped forward. 'Our friend has been caught by the swamp monster.'

'We think he's been eaten,' said Hare.

'We need to save him,' said Fox.

The witch frowned. 'Hmm. Where is this monster?'

'In the cave,' said Fox. 'Mouse was dragged inside.'

'Humph!' she said, pulling the waistband of her trousers up higher. 'Well, no good

standing around. I'll just have to take a look myself.'

'Can you put a spell on it?' asked Willow.

'Eh?' said the witch.

'A spell, or curse,' insisted Willow. 'You are a witch after all, aren't you?'

The witch gave Willow a curious look. She ran her hand over her matted hair. 'If you say so.'

'It's big,' said Fox, 'with huge teeth.'

'Tell me,' said the witch. 'Have you heard it howl?'

Willow nodded. 'Last night and today.'

The witch nodded thoughtfully. 'Hmm. I thought so. I did too.' She walked towards the mouth of the cave, but before she reached it, the monster padded out of the shadows with Mouse's sword between its teeth.

And Mouse was walking by its side.

'I've made friends with the swamp monster,' said Mouse, a big grin on his face.

'We thought you'd been eaten,' said Hare.

'He's very friendly,' said Mouse. 'His name's Colin.'

'Colin?' said Raven. 'How do you know?'

'There's a metal disc hanging around his neck with his name on it,' said Mouse.

The witch bent down to have a look. 'Hmm. You're right. I think we need to bring this monster back to my hut and find out what sort he really is.'

'Wait a minute,' said Hare. 'I want to look for my compass and Fox's penknife. They went missing from our camp.' She went into the cave and came out with a puzzled expression. 'They're not there.'

'Are you sure?' said Fox. He went to look too.

But the penknife and compass were nowhere to be seen.

Willow turned to the witch. 'How did you get across the swamp?'

The witch pointed at the swamp. 'I often come this way to pick mushrooms. I've laid a path of planks across the bog. You'll have to follow me.'

The pathway made from planks was slightly submerged below the water, invisible to those who didn't know it was there, but it held their weight. Willow and the Wild Things, Sniff, and Colin followed the witch to her hut in the clearing. Back at the witch's camp, a blackened cauldron was hanging over the ashes of a fire.

'A real witch's cauldron,' whispered
Mouse, impressed. He peered into it, his eyes
widening. 'Do you make potions?'

'Of sorts,' said the witch.

'You're not going to eat us?' asked Mouse.

'You're lucky,' said the witch. 'I've had lunch
already.' She filled the cauldron with water
from a big water butt that held rainwater. 'I'm
going to make a transformation potion for the
swamp monster.'

'Cool,' said Mouse.

The witch dipped her finger in the water.
'A bit cold, I think. I'll light the fire to warm it
up, and you can sit here and warm up too.'

The witch busied herself lighting the fire,
and the flames licked and curled around the
cauldron. 'A bit of lavender,' she said, tossing a

sprig of leaves into the cauldron. She stirred it around. 'And some washing-up liquid.'

'Washing-up liquid?' said Hare. 'What sort of potion is this?'

'Wait and see,' said the witch.

Colin the swamp monster lay down next to the fire, the wet mud hardening into a thick shell on his body.

Willow stared into the flames. 'Are you really a witch?'

'We thought you were a writer,' said Hare.

Bear leaned closer. 'Do you write powerful magic spells?'

'I suppose all words are powerful. But are they magic?' said the witch.

Mouse peered at the witch. 'You don't look much like a witch. You have the crooked nose, but you don't have a pointy hat or any warts.'

The witch raised an eyebrow. 'I'm a young witch, actually. I'm only fifty. Most witches don't get warts until they're at least two hundred years old.'

'Can you turn Fox into a frog?' asked Raven with a wicked smile.

'I don't do gimmicks,' said the witch.

'What do you do?' asked Fox.

The witch was silent for a moment, her hands beneath her chin. 'It's a good question,' she said. 'I suppose you could say I conjure openings into other worlds.'

'Like magic doorways?' said Willow. 'Where do you go?'

'Anywhere I want,' said the witch. 'I can walk in steamy jungles or tread on frozen icebergs. I can open up windows into the past or the future. I can slip between the folds in the universe to parallel worlds.'

'But how do you know any of it is real?' asked Bear.

The witch frowned. 'How do any of us know anything is real?'

Bear scratched his head and frowned.

The witch leaned forward. 'If you can imagine it, then why can't it be real?'

Mouse stared around, wide-eyed. 'Did you make the opening into the Wilderness?'

'The Wilderness?' said the witch.

'Yes, this place,' said Raven.

The witch looked up at the trees and the branches swaying in the breeze and the light dancing on the forest floor. A woodpecker drummed on a tree trunk, and insects hummed in the canopy of leaves. 'The Wilderness is already in this world,' she said. 'People only need to open their eyes to see it. These woods hold the deepest form of magic. It weaves its way into your soul. It binds you and connects you to this earth.'

Steam began to swirl up from the cauldron, and the witch rolled up her sleeve and dipped her elbow in. 'Perfect. Not too warm and not too cold. Now hold Colin tight. We're going to try a bit of a transformation.'

The witch tipped the contents of the cauldron over Colin. Warm water ran over him, soaking into the mud.

The witch stood back. 'If I were you, I'd take cover!'

Colin put his nose in the air and began to shake his head from side to side, slowly at first, but then faster and faster until his

whole body was shaking and spraying mud
and water into the air.

Colin finished with a shake of his long
tail, and stood transformed into the biggest,
shaggiest yellow dog that Willow had ever
seen.

Chapter 12
Colin Goes Home

'A dog!' said Mouse. 'That was cool.'

'He's not a monster at all,' said Fox, sounding disappointed.

'Apparently not,' said the witch.

'So it was him that was howling,' said Hare. 'Because he was lost.'

'I thought it sounded sad and lonely,' said Willow.

'He's been out all night,' said the witch. 'I expect he's a bit cold.'

Willow reached into her rucksack.
'He can have my fleece blanket,' she said,
wrapping it around him. Colin gave her
cheek a lick.

The witch nodded. 'We're all a bit cold.
I'll stoke up the fire and put on some more
water to heat up.'

Raven shuffled nearer to the fire and
put her arm around Colin. 'Do you think
someone owns him?'

'Oh, I expect so,' said the witch. 'He's got
a collar and a name.'

'I'll take him home,' said Hare. 'Whoever
owns him shouldn't have been so careless to
lose him.'

'I think his owner would probably like
him back very much,' said the witch. 'I'll try
to call them here.'

'With a summoning charm?' asked
Mouse.

'No, with my phone,' said the witch. She
bent down to look at the disc on the collar.
'The phone number is on the other side.'

The witch went into her hut to talk
on the phone. Mumbled conversation
drifted through the door. They heard
something about children, a lost dog, and
marshmallows.

The Wild Things huddled closer to the
fire, watching the flames leap higher and
crackle in the late afternoon. Sniff yawned
and curled up next to Willow at her feet.
Bear and Hare yawned loudly too. Mouse
tucked himself under one of Raven's wings.

The witch came out of her hut. 'The
owners are on their way,' she said. 'They've

missed him very much.'

'Oh!' said Hare, sounding disappointed. 'I wish we could keep him.'

'He'll be glad to get home,' said the witch. 'He's had quite an adventure. He'll have lots of tales to tell. So will you.'

Fox folded his arms and stared into the fire. 'There were strange blue flames over the swamp,' he said. 'I wonder what they were. Maybe I imagined them.'

'They might have been will-o'-the-wisps,' said the witch. 'Some say they are malevolent spirits that lure people into the swamp. They are sometimes called the Fool's Fire.'

Fox went a little red at hearing that. They had fooled him too.

'Uff!' barked Sniff, waking from his

snooze. He pricked up his ears and turned to look along the track.

Colin sat up too, sniffing the air and wagging his tail.

'Now, excuse me while I get my coat,' said the witch. She went into her hut and came out wearing a long black coat. She fastened the buttons, covering her bright shirt and trousers. 'People always seem a little alarmed to see a woman my age wearing brightly coloured clothes sitting by a campfire.'

Mouse nodded. 'I suppose Outsiders can't tell you're a witch,' he said. 'They'll just think you're a weird woman in the woods.'

The witch raised an eyebrow and said nothing.

'Outsiders can't see the Wilderness either,' said Raven.

'Shh!' said the witch, putting her finger to her mouth. 'Here come Colin's owners.'

The Outsiders came hurrying along the track into the clearing. When Colin saw them, he bounded over to them, almost knocking them down.

Colin's owners were a middle-aged couple. 'You gave us such a fright, Colin,' said the woman.

'Thank you for finding him,' said the man. 'He was chasing a bird and pulled me over. I lost grip of him, and he just disappeared. We thought something terrible had happened to him. We've been searching for days.'

The witch nodded. 'And it's thanks to these children who heard him and rescued him that he's safe.'

The woman turned to them. 'Now, I heard that you might be in need of a hot drink after your adventures.' She reached into a bag and pulled out a tub of hot chocolate powder and two packets of marshmallows. 'This is from Colin to say thank you.'

'Thank you,' said Willow. She gave Colin a huge hug. 'If he ever gets lost in here again, we'll let you know.'

The man looked around the trees and shivered. 'It's a shame about this place.' He pointed to an old rusty bicycle at the end of the track. 'People just dump rubbish in here. It needs a good tidy-up.'

'Come on, now,' said the woman, ushering her husband along the track. 'Colin needs his supper. I expect he's hungry.'

'I doubt Colin's hungry,' said Bear, watching them leave. 'He ate all our doughnuts.'

The witch put her hands on her hips. 'They were very rude about my bicycle. It might be old and rusty, but it still works.'

'But they did give us hot chocolate and marshmallows,' said Hare.

'Yes,' agreed the witch. 'And I think that'll be the best potion for us all.'

Chapter 13
Monsters and Marshmallows

The witch poured hot chocolate for everyone and handed out clean sticks for the Wild Things to toast marshmallows.

The campfire settled into a warm orange glow.

Willow cupped her hands around her warm mug and smiled. Her hands were grubby, her feet were muddy, and her hair was tangled and smelled of wood smoke, but she felt happier than she had been for a long time. She wished that Freddie could be here too.

Bear held his marshmallow over the fire and watched the sugar burn brown. 'Are there really monsters?'

'Possibly,' said the witch. 'The worst ones are the invisible ones that whisper in our ear. Sometimes they tell us we are not good enough, and sometimes they make us jealous or angry.'

Fox stared into his mug. 'I was jealous of Raven and her ideas. I only went across the bog because I wanted to show I was the leader. I should have listened to her.'

Raven hung her head. 'I was angry at Mouse when I shouldn't have been. If I was a good leader, I wouldn't have abandoned him when he couldn't cross the ravine.'

'And I should teach you all about the wild signs,' said Hare. 'I don't because I want you to think I'm the best at it.'

Willow looked across at her. 'So how did you know which way was north when we were in the woods?'

'I'd noticed the direction of the wind before,' said Hare. 'It was coming from the south and pushing the clouds north, so I could tell just by looking at the way the clouds were blowing.'

'That's so cool,' said Willow. 'I'd love to know all about the wild signs.'

Hare smiled shyly. 'I could teach you all.'

'I think I've got an invisible monster too,' whispered Mouse. 'It told me I wasn't brave. I believed it until I found my new sword.

But I don't have it now. Colin broke it.'

'It's not the sword that made you brave,' said Willow. 'You were brave when you believed you were brave.'

Mouse turned to Willow. 'Do you have an invisible monster?'

Willow hugged her knees against her chest. 'I have worries that won't go away. I want my little brother to come out of hospital again. That's why I'm collecting things to show him, so he can look forward to playing with me in our new garden.' She pulled out the snail shell from her pocket. 'I don't have anything else to show him yet.'

'We can help you with that,' said Hare. She pulled the stub of her pencil from her pocket. 'Give Freddie this. It has drawn the map of the Wilderness. Tell him there's

magic inside it.'

Mouse scooped some mud into his hand and shaped it into a ball. He poked eye holes with a stick. 'This is a model swamp monster. You can tell Freddie all about our adventures.'

Bear handed Willow a stick. 'This is my marshmallow toasting stick. He can keep it and use it to toast marshmallows when he comes here.'

Fox picked an acorn from the ground. 'Freddie can have this from me. Tell him it holds a whole tree inside it ready to grow.'

'We'd like to meet him,' said Raven. She plucked a feather from her cloak. 'Tell him

this is his pass into the Wilderness.'

Willow put the gifts into her pockets and smiled.

Mouse turned to the witch. 'How do you fight invisible monsters?'

The witch glugged back the last of her hot chocolate. 'You ignore them,' she said. 'You don't feed them with what they want. You find a stronger power. And you're lucky to have that.'

'What's that?' asked Hare.

'What saved you in the end?' asked the witch.

Hare frowned. 'Well, we all did it. Together.'

'Exactly,' smiled the witch. 'You are friends. You have each other.'

Chapter 14
The Best Adventure

The shadows began to lengthen across the forest floor, and Willow shivered.

'Well,' said the witch. 'My work here is done for the day. I must leave.'

'We need to go too,' said Raven. 'It's later than we thought.'

The witch led the Wild Things back to the path to River Camp.

Sniff was so tired that Willow carried him in her rucksack.

'Thank you for helping to save me,' said Bear to Willow. 'I'm glad the Wild Things met you and Sniff. That was the best adventure ever.'

As the Wild Things neared River Camp, a chill crept into the air. Everything looked normal, but it was strangely quiet.

'Uff!' warned Sniff.

'There's no birdsong,' said Raven. She walked slowly into the middle of the camp and looked around.

The others followed.

Fox sniffed. 'Something's different. Someone's been here.'

Hare crouched low and traced her fingers along the ground. 'There are fresh prints,' she said. She looked up and squinted into the light slanting through the trees. 'The

prints are going towards the Forest of
Forever Night.'

'Whoever they are, they've gone now.
Let's rebuild our den before we go home,'
said Fox. 'I don't like to think of it ruined
here.'

Willow helped the Wild Things repair
the den. She used her skipping rope to lash
together the branches to hold the tarpaulin

in place.

'There,' said Raven. 'It's ready for us to return.'

Hare sat on the ground with the map spread out before her. She found a new pencil and drew the swamp on to the map and the witch's track across it. She pushed the map into its tube and hid it in a hollow tree trunk for safekeeping.

'I'm glad Colin wasn't really a scary monster after all,' said Mouse.

'I still don't understand what happened to my compass,' said Hare.

'Or my penknife,' said Fox.

'Colin couldn't have taken them,' said Bear. 'He's a dog.'

'Well, I can't see anything missing today,' said Raven, picking up blankets and folding them into the box in the den.

Fox picked up the tin of emergency chocolate and looked inside. His face turned from surprise to anger. 'It's empty,' he said, showing the others. 'It was full before we left for the swamp. So it couldn't have been Colin. Someone or something has definitely been here since.'

Mouse's eyes opened wide. 'So we're not

the only ones in the Wilderness?'

'It's a mystery,' said Hare. 'A mystery we'll have to come back and solve.'

Bear stared into the darkness between the trees. 'It's been the best adventure,' he said. 'And the best adventures always have another one waiting for them at the other end.'

Chapter 15
Willow Wildthing

Willow and Sniff followed the Wild Things back through the tunnel of thorns to the Green Slime River.

Hare turned to Willow. 'Are you going to come with us again?'

'I'd like to,' said Willow.

'Good,' said Raven. 'You have to. You're a Wild Thing now.'

'She needs a name,' said Mouse.

'I'm Willow,' said Willow.

'I mean a Wild Thing name,' said Mouse.

'I'm not really called Mouse.'

'What's your real name?' asked Willow.

'It doesn't matter what our real names are,' said Fox. 'It matters what our wild name is.'

Mouse put his head to one side. 'Your wild name must suit you.'

Willow pulled at some willow leaves that had stuck to her hair when she was swinging across the bog.

'You look better with them in,' said Hare.

Raven nodded. 'I've got an idea. Time for a Wild Squawk!'

Willow watched as the Wild Things huddled together and chatted, occasionally looking up at her. Then they all stood in a line and faced her.

'We've decided,' said Raven.

The others nodded.

Raven reached over and pulled out a strand of willow that had been caught in Willow's hair. She curled it into a bracelet and slid it on to Willow's wrist.

'You don't need to change your name. It suits you as it is. We name you Willow,' said Fox. 'Willow Wildthing.'

Willow smiled.

Mouse took her hand. 'You're one of us now.'

'Uff!' barked Sniff.

Fox patted him on the head. 'You're a Wild Thing too.'

But Sniff was barking at something else.

'Willow! Willow . . . where are you?'

'That's my mum,' said Willow. 'I need

to get across Green Slime River before she sees me.'

The Wild Things crossed just in time, and Raven pulled up the drawbridge. They all pulled on their shoes, and, as they did, they seemed to change. Fox became less foxy. Raven's wings fell in loose cloth at her side. Hare seemed to be less bouncy, and Mouse lost his twitchy nose. Bear's tummy seemed to shrink too.

'Don't worry,' said Raven. 'We'll change back when we enter the Wilderness again.'

'See you,' said Mouse, giving her a wave goodbye.

Willow watched them walk away. Her mind was filled with so many questions. Who were they? Where did they live? When were they coming back?

'There you are!' said Willow's mum, hurrying along the path. 'I was worried about you. You know we don't like you going off by yourself. You were gone for ages.'

'I was just playing,' said Willow. 'I made some friends.'

'You'll need a bath,' said Mum. 'You look like you've been dragged through a hedge. Sniff too. What have you been doing?'

'Uff!' said Sniff.

And Willow was glad for the first time that Sniff couldn't talk.

At home, Willow laid out all her treasures.

'What have you got there?' asked Dad.

'Things I found for Freddie,' said Willow.

Mum peered over. 'Some of those are a bit small. He might try to put them in his mouth.'

Willow sighed. 'I wanted to show them to him.' Secretly, she wanted to tell him all about her adventures in the Wilderness.

'I've got an idea,' said Dad. He went outside and came back with two sticks and a piece of string. 'We can make a mobile to hang over his bed so he can look at them. You can take it to him tomorrow.'

Willow tied the feather and the marshmallow toasting stick and the acorn and all the other things the Wild Things had given her to the mobile. She imagined Freddie looking up at them while the mobile spun in the breeze. One day she

would take him to the Wilderness. Maybe the magic from it would seep into Freddie too.

That night, at bedtime, Willow switched out the light. She pulled on her dressing gown and opened the window as wide as she could. She hugged Sniff against her chest and stood with him, staring out. A pale silvery mist lay like a blanket over the trees, and somewhere an owl hooted into the night.

It had been scary moving to a different house in a different town.

But she had found new friends and a new world to explore.

She was now part of the Wilderness.

She couldn't wait to go back.

She was Willow Wildthing.

And out there were adventures just waiting for her to return.

How to make your own den!

You can make your very own den, just like the Wild Things. You could use it as a meeting place, a camp-out, somewhere to read . . . the possibilities are endless!

You will need:

- rope/old washing line
- blanket/tarpaulin
- tent pegs
- cushions

1. Choose a suitable patch of grass between two trees. Make sure there aren't any loose branches—you don't want them to fall off the tree and on to your den (or you!).

2. Run a rope or an old piece of washing line between the trees and secure it to the trunks, being careful not to damage the trees.

3. Drape a blanket or a tarpaulin over the rope.

4. Peg one side of the blanket to the ground.

5. Finally, decorate your den! You can use blankets, cushions, a torch. Anything you can find to make it feel comfortable.

Gill Lewis spent much of her childhood in the garden, where she ran a small zoo and a veterinary hospital for creepy-crawlies, mice, and birds. When she grew up she became a real vet and travelled from the Arctic to Africa in search of interesting animals and places.

Gill now writes books for children. Her previous novels have published to worldwide critical acclaim and have been translated into more than twenty languages.

She lives in the depths of Somerset with her husband and three children and writes from a tree house in the company of squirrels.

Rebecca Bagley is a children's book illustrator in the south-west of England.

Illustrators are funny sort of grown-up. They do grown-up things, like brushing their teeth (every day), but they also sit around drawing pictures and then call it a job. Recently, Rebecca has been drawing a lot of leaves, as well as all the magical things that live amongst them, and she couldn't be happier about it.

In between drawings, Rebecca daydreams about having her own garden one day, where she will grow tomatoes, practise handstands, and have a really big dog. Until then, she entertains herself and her little family by feeding new and weird flavours to her baby girl who, so far, has been a very good sport.

Ready for more great stories?
Try one of these …